THE MOVIE STORYBOOK

JURASSIC PARK

TM & © 1993 UNIVERSAL CITY STUDIOS, INC. & AMBLIN ENTERTAINMENT, INC.

GROSSET & DUNLAP

Adapted by JANE MASON

From a screenplay by MICHAEL CRICHTON
and DAVID KOEPP

Based on the novel by MICHAEL CRICHTON

TM & © 1993 Universal Studios, Inc. & Amblin Entertainment, Inc. All rights reserved. JURASSIC PARK and the JURASSIC PARK logo are registered trademarks of Universal City Studios, Inc. & Amblin Entertainment, Inc. Published by Grosset & Dunlap, Inc., a member of The Putnam & Grosset Group, New York. Published simultaneously in Canada. Printed in the U.S.A. Library of Congress Catalog Card Number: 92-74985   ISBN 0-448-40173-8
A B C D E F G H I J

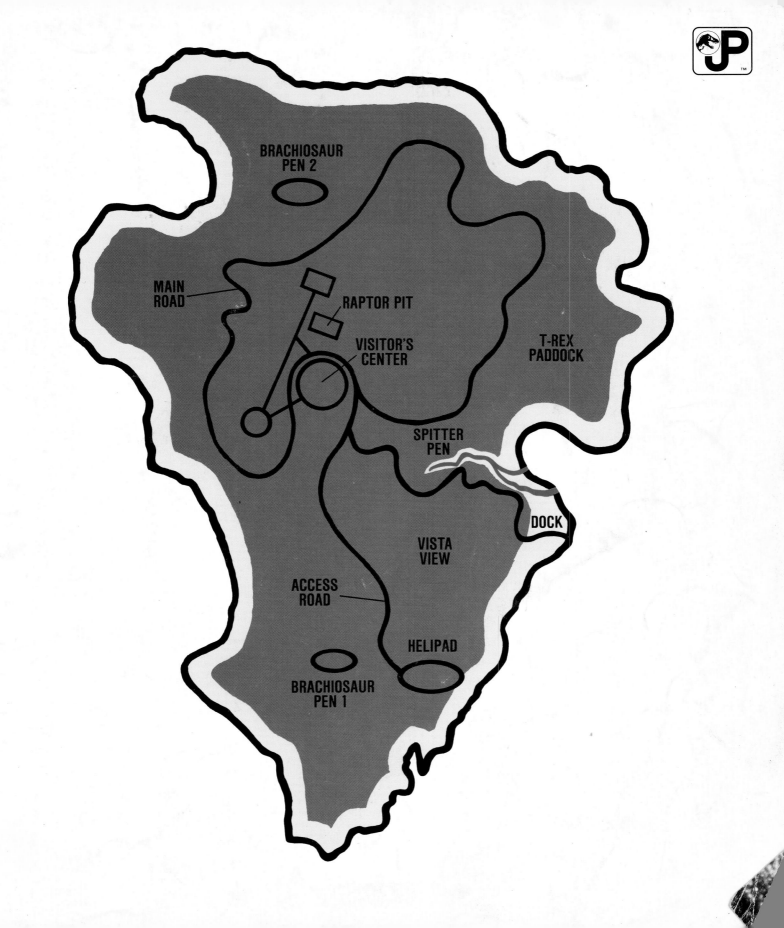

In the Pacific Ocean, not far from Costa Rica, lies an island called Isla Nublar. Nobody lives on this island, and a heavy mist covers the lush green vines and trees that grow there.

The native people of Costa Rica speak of Isla Nublar in hushed whispers. Not because of the eerie fog and the dark, remote jungle that cover the island, but because of an amazing and terrible thing that happened there....

Far away from Isla Nublar, in the Montana badlands, an archaeological dig was going on. Dr. Alan Grant, a famous paleontologist, had just found a fourth Velociraptor skeleton. The Velociraptor was a small dinosaur. But it was very fierce and intelligent.

Alan Grant's assistant, Dr. Ellie Sattler, helped him chip chunks of earth away from the fragile, ancient bones.

"That's the fourth complete skeleton we've found in this area," Alan said. "They must have died together."

"Then they lived together, too, right?" Ellie asked.

"Yes, and they hunted in packs." He looked puzzled. "But what killed them?"

Suddenly the wind whipped up all around them, blowing sand and dirt everywhere. A helicopter was descending on the camp.

"Cover everything!" Alan shouted to the volunteers who were working on the dig. "Fast!" He shook his fist at the helicopter. "Lunatic!" he cried. Didn't they know that the sand could ruin the fragile fossils? Months of hard work could be lost! He headed toward camp to find out what this unexpected intrusion was all about.

Start "What do you think you're doing?" Alan stormed into a camp trailer where a visitor was waiting.

"John Hammond," the man introduced himself. "I'm pleased to finally meet you, Dr. Grant."

"Did you say *Hammond*?" Alan could barely get the words out. This was the wealthy man who had funded his work for four years!

As soon as Ellie arrived and was introduced, Mr. Hammond got down to business. "I'll get right to the point," he began. "I own an island off the coast of Costa Rica. I've been setting up a kind of biological preserve there. I hope to open it to the public next year, but I've got a problem. There's this lawyer—a real worrywart. He represents my investors. And they don't think it's safe. So I need you two to come see it. You know, give it your stamp of approval."

Alan was confused. "Why us?" he asked.

Mr. Hammond smiled. "Let's just say that it's right up your alley. I want you to come down for the weekend."

At the airport in Costa Rica, Alan, Ellie, and Mr. Hammond met up with two other people. One was the lawyer Mr. Hammond had been complaining about. His name was Donald Gennaro, and he looked nervous. The other was Dr. Ian Malcolm. He was a scientist, too. A mathematician. And he didn't seem too optimistic about Mr. Hammond's island.

From the airport, all five adults boarded a helicopter that would take them to Isla Nublar.

"Hold on!" the helicopter pilot shouted near the end of the flight. "The landing could be a bit rough."

Alan looked out the window just as the island came into view. Its jagged cliffs rose straight out of the water and the jungle foliage was covered with thick clouds.

"Welcome to Jurassic Park," Mr. Hammond said excitedly as the helicopter touched ground.

Two Jeeps were waiting to take the guests to the main compound. As they drove along the mountain roads, Alan and Ellie stared in surprise at their surroundings. There were huge electric fences and giant concrete moats everywhere. But that's not what surprised them the most. Everything looked like it belonged to another time—the island seemed prehistoric!

In an open area of the park, Alan noticed a strange, gray tree trunk. He looked up…and up some more, and his jaw dropped. It was no tree trunk! It was a dinosaur leg!

Then Ellie saw it, too. She was too shocked to say anything.

When Ian Malcolm spotted the dinosaur, he just shook his head. "Are you crazy?" he said to Mr. Hammond. "That's a *dinosaur*. You think you can control a beast like that? Man and dinosaurs aren't *supposed* to live together."

Mr. Hammond didn't hear what Ian was saying. He was too busy listening to Alan and Ellie.

"Look at the way it moves," Ellie said.

"It must be warm-blooded!" Alan went on. "We were right! How long is that neck?" He turned to Mr. Hammond. "Twenty-five feet?"

"Thirty," he answered.

"Are there more dinosaurs?" Alan wanted to know.

"Of course," Mr. Hammond nodded. "Let's go on to the Visitor's Center."

"We're going to make a fortune off this place," Gennaro said. He didn't look nervous anymore. Instead, his eyes were full of greed. "A *fortune*."

"How did you do it?" Alan asked.

"You'll soon find out," answered Mr. Hammond.

The main compound was fenced in from the rest of the park. Inside, there was a large building that would be the Visitor's Center.

As the Jeeps pulled up to the center, they passed an impressive cage that seemed to need high security.

The lobby of the Center wasn't finished yet, but two giant dinosaur skeletons, a Tyrannosaur and a Brachiosaur, stood in the middle of it.

The group followed Mr. Hammond into a theater and everyone took a seat. As the lights dimmed, a strange-looking character appeared on a screen. It looked like two pieces of string wound together.

"Hi," the character said. "I'm Mr. DNA. Just one drop of your blood contains billions of strands of DNA, the building blocks of life.

"You see," Mr. DNA went on, "mosquitos lived when dinosaurs lived. And sometimes, after biting a dinosaur and filling up on its blood, a mosquito would get stuck in the sap on the branch of a tree. When the sap got hard and turned into amber, the mosquito was preserved, blood and all, inside."

"Wait a minute..." Alan called out. He knew it couldn't really be that simple. "How did you..."

Eau Claire District Library

Mr. DNA kept talking. "Then our scientists took the blood from the mosquitos and, BINGO. They had dino DNA. And if there were any holes, they just filled them in with frog DNA, because most animal DNA is 90 percent identical."

Suddenly the auditorium seats began to move out of the theater and into a laboratory. Scientists in white coats bustled around. In one area there were rows of large eggs, and a baby dinosaur was just breaking out of one.

Alan got out of his seat and went to pick up the tiny creature.

"Perfect timing," Mr. Hammond said.

"I've been here for the hatching of every animal on the island."

"Surely not the ones that have been born in the wild," Ian Malcolm said. "You couldn't have been there for those hatchings."

"Oh, they can't breed in the wild," Mr. Hammond said firmly. "They're all female."

"Population control is one of our safety features," added one of the scientists. "There is no unauthorized breeding on this island."

Ellie and Ian looked suspicious. They didn't believe what the scientist said for a second. But Alan was busy studying the

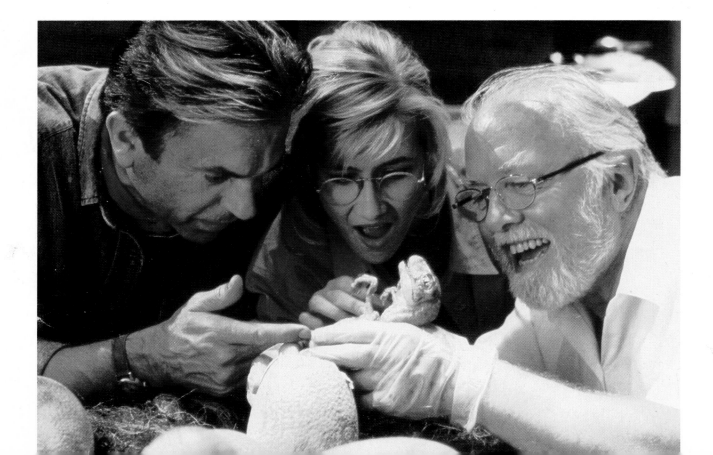

baby dinosaur, his face dark with concern.

"What species is this?" he asked.

"It's a Velociraptor," the scientist answered.

"You bred *Raptors*?" Alan asked in shock. He couldn't believe that they would take that kind of risk. "Are there others?"

"There's plenty of time to see the Raptors, Dr. Grant," Mr. Hammond said as he followed Alan to the heavily secured cage they had passed on the way in. "Why don't we have some lunch?"

Lunch? No way. Alan was intent on seeing the Raptors.

The thick plants around the bars of the Raptor cage made it impossible to see anything, but it was easy to hear the vicious snarls that came from inside.

Alan leaned in close to the bars and Ellie put her arm on his. "They're not bones anymore," she said.

"Why can't we see them?" Alan asked.

"We're, uh, still perfecting the viewing system." Mr. Hammond looked uncomfortable. "The Raptors aren't adjusting to being in a park setting very well."

"They should all be destroyed." Robert Muldoon, the park's game warden, joined the group. "They're lethal at six months and are incredible jumpers."

"Oh, you're an alarmist," Mr. Hammond interrupted, leading the group away from the Velociraptor pen. "Let's have some lunch."

After lunch, Mr. Hammond told his guests that they'd be taking a tour of the island. "And you're going to have a little company out in the park," he said as two children came running into the lobby. "These are my grandchildren," he said proudly. "Tim and Lex."

Alan rolled his eyes. "Kids," he muttered under his breath. "Noisy, messy, smelly kids."

"Kids are not smelly, Alan," Ellie said as she went to greet the newest arrivals. She introduced herself to Lex and the two seemed to hit it off instantly.

As it turned out, Tim was a real dinosaur buff and had read Alan's book. Soon Tim was talking his ear off about dinosaur evolution, Alan's specialty.

The most exciting feature about Jurassic Park was going to be the dinosaur tour. Electric cars ran along a track, stopping to show the visitors each dinosaur on the island.

As soon as they had all climbed into the tour cars, Lex started fiddling with a computer screen. "Wow!" she said. "This is an interactive CD-ROM. It talks."

"She's a computer nerd," Tim explained to Donald Gennaro, who was riding in the same car.

"I'm a *hacker*," she said defensively.

The cars moved along the tour path. When they stopped at the Tyrannosaurus rex paddock, everyone looked eagerly for the dinosaur while the computer rambled on about the ferocious hunter. But the dinosaur was a no-show.

Then, suddenly, Alan saw something move in the distance. In a flash he was out of the car heading toward it, with the others trailing behind.

Donald looked around nervously. "We shouldn't be doing this," he said. "I'm sure it's not safe."

But nobody listened.

"Cool!" Alan and Tim said at the same time. They were standing right in front of a full-grown Triceratops. The dinosaur was lying on its side and it took Alan only a minute to see that she was ill. Her dark purple tongue was covered with blisters.

"It looks like some kind of poison," Ellie said. "Those berries are poisonous." She pointed to a clump of strange-looking berry bushes. "But I don't think she'd eat them."

"Hey, look," Tim said to Alan. He was pointing to a pile of smooth stones on the ground. "I've seen pictures of these in your book."

Ellie stooped down and picked up one of the smooth rocks. Suddenly her eyes lit up. "It's the gizzard stones!" she said.

The others looked confused, so she went on. "The Triceratops eats rocks to help mash her food. But over time the rocks in her stomach get worn smooth and don't work anymore. So she throws them up and eats more rocks. But when she ate these rocks near the bushes, I'll bet she accidentally ate the poisonous berries, too," she finished.

Alan nodded.

"Hmmmm," Tim said thoughtfully.

"That's pretty neat."

Suddenly lightning flashed and everyone realized that the sky was darkening.

Ellie decided to stay for a while and help with the sick Triceratops, but the rest of the group hurried back to the cars.

Back in the control room, Mr. Hammond and his computer expert, Dennis Nedry, were watching the group on video screens.

"There's a tropical storm coming," said Ray Arnold, another of Mr. Hammond's computer workers. "It's going to be a big one."

"We'll have to call off the rest of the tour," Mr. Hammond said. But Dennis wasn't listening. He was programming the computer to shut down for a while. He needed all the doors to unlock so he could get into the fertilization lab. He was going to steal dinosaur embryos and sell them on the mainland.

A few minutes later, in the park, the tour cars jerked to a halt near the edge of a cliff. The computer screens went blank. Then rain began to thunder down from the sky.

"Blackout!" said Tim excitedly. He pulled some night-vision goggles out from under the seat and put them on. Then, suddenly, he heard an echoing, booming sound—like giant footsteps. "Do you hear that?" he asked Lex and Donald.

They both nodded slowly, their eyes wide with fear.

The thundering echo was getting louder and louder.

Tim looked up through the car's sunroof and saw the Tyrannosaurus rex looming above them. It was clutching the "electrified" fence. With the power off, the fence wouldn't keep the dinosaur inside!

DANGER
10,000
VOLTS

When Donald saw the T-rex, he screamed, jumped out of the car, and took off. The dinosaur saw the movement and chewed his way through the fence in a second.

Donald's heart pounded in his chest as he ran. The Tyrannosaur's footsteps seemed to come from everywhere at once. A small, unfinished shelter was just ahead, and Donald threw himself through the door just in time.

Lex and Tim huddled in their car, shaking, as a huge yellow eye peered at them through the windshield. The Tyrannosaur pushed, tipping the car over, and the glass windows shattered. Then the car lurched to the side and the kids were thrown against the doors.

The T-rex started to nudge the car toward the barrier. Then it sunk its teeth into the metal and shook the car from side to side.

Alan watched from inside the other car. When the T-rex shook the car, he knew it was time to make his move. He jumped out of the car and shouted at the dinosaur from the middle of the road. "Hey!" He waved a flare with bright flames shooting out of one end, "Over *here*."

Ian Malcolm watched Alan for a minute. Then he bolted into the night, running down the road to the shelter where Donald was hiding. The T-rex turned away from the cars, chased after him, and flicked him into the air with his nose. Ian sailed right through a wood portion of the wall into the shelter. He

was injured and unable to get up.

Then the T-rex burst through the wall of the shelter. Alan heard Donald scream from inside. Then everything was quiet.

Alan scrambled over to the car and pulled Lex out. "Tim is knocked out," Lex whispered frantically. Then the T-rex was right there. Its huge leg slammed down in front of them. Right behind them was a cliff. They were trapped!

"Don't move!" Alan said. "It can't see us if we don't move."

Lex stood completely still while the T-rex sniffed the car. Then the huge dinosaur bent down and peered through the broken sunroof. Tim woke up and screamed, desperately trying to back away from the hole in the roof. He wedged himself between two seats just as the T-rex stretched its long tongue into the car. Tim kicked at the tongue wildly and the T-rex lifted its head and roared in anger.

Frustrated, the T-rex took one last lunge at the car. It rolled forward, straight toward Alan and Lex. At the last moment, Alan grabbed Lex and put her on his back. He started to climb down the cliff, using a broken fence cable to help him along.

The T-rex watched them from the top of the cliff, roaring in frustration once

again. Then it turned back to the car with Tim inside and hurled it over the cliff.

"Timmy!" Lex screamed as the car tumbled over the edge. It fell several feet, then landed on a thick tree branch.

In another part of the park, Dennis Nedry was escaping with his stolen embryos. If he could just get his cargo to the boat at the dock, he'd be a rich man.

The rain poured down as he drove along the muddy park road. Suddenly there was a cement wall blocking his way! Dennis slammed on the brakes and the car skidded out of control, swerving into a muddy ditch. "I've got to make it to the boat," he told himself. He grabbed a flashlight and got out of the car to investigate.

Dennis shone his flashlight on the rear wheels of the Jeep. They were stuck in six inches of mud.

Suddenly there was an eerie hooting in the distance. But when Dennis looked up he saw only darkness.

DILOPHOSAURUS

As the hooting came closer, Dennis turned to see a strange-looking dinosaur coming toward him. It was a Dilophosaur. It hopped around Dennis playfully.

"Shoo," Dennis said. "Go home."

But the Dilophosaur wanted to play. "Hoot, hoot," it said.

"You're in my way," Dennis shouted. He didn't have time for this. "Go on!"

The dinosaur just kept hopping around and hooting. Finally, Dennis threw a small rock at it. The Dilophosaur stared at Dennis for a few moments. Then it reared its head back and spat, hitting Dennis right in the face.

Suddenly Dennis's face started to burn. He couldn't see. He stumbled to the driver's side of the car and climbed

inside. But as soon as he shut the door he realized that he wasn't alone. The Dilophosaur was in the car, too, ready to attack.

On the other side of the park, Alan climbed up to the car resting in the tree. Inside, Tim was huddled on the floor.

"I threw up," he said, embarrassed.

"That's okay," Alan said. "Why don't you come out of there and climb down with me?"

Tim didn't budge. He was too afraid to move. Finally, after a lot of coaxing, he crawled out of the car.

As they scrambled from limb to limb, the branch supporting the car began to creak and groan. Then the car began to fall.

Alan and Tim climbed down as fast as they could, but the car was gaining speed as it fell from branch to branch above them. In a panic, they jumped the last few feet to the ground and rolled away from the tree. A split second later the car smashed to the ground on top of them. They were saved by the hole in the sunroof!

Back at the Visitor's Center, Ellie, Robert Muldoon, and Mr. Hammond knew that things were going from bad to worse. Dennis had rigged the computer system and now everything was jammed. Even the electrified

The two headed into the park in a gas-powered Jeep.

When they came to the place where the cars had stopped during the blackout, Ellie and Robert were horrified. Everyone was gone—even the kids. One of the

fences were off. And that meant that the dinosaurs—even the Tyrannosaurus rex—were roaming everywhere.

"Go get my grandkids," Mr. Hammond said to Robert.

Robert nodded.

"I'm going with you," Ellie insisted.

cars was missing. And a shelter a short distance away had been destroyed.

Ellie ran to the shelter and began looking for clues. Where were Alan and the kids? She started to poke through the rubble. She heard the T-rex roar in the distance. She looked around, frightened.

Then Ellie heard a soft moaning. It was Ian. He lay on the ground. He was injured and in pain.

"Let's get him into the Jeep," Robert said. Ellie was close to tears, but she nodded and helped lift Ian into the car.

After Ian was settled on the backseat, Robert put a comforting arm around Ellie's shoulder. "I've seen a lot of animal attacks," he said. "People just disappear without any clues."

Ellie jerked away from Robert and walked over to the tour car. She flashed her light inside but it was empty. There had to be something—something to tell her that Alan and the kids were still alive. Then she noticed deep ruts in the ground near the edge of the cliff. She walked to the edge and shone her flashlight into the darkness.

"The other car!" she called to Robert and Ian as the beam sprayed light inside the wrecked vehicle.

Just then the T-rex roared and a rhythmic pounding echoed through the jungle. A second later the T-rex smashed through the trees, charging after them. Ellie jumped into the Jeep and Robert hit the gas, hard. The Jeep thundered ahead, getting away just in time.

Alan, Tim, and Lex walked all afternoon, trying to get back to the Visitors' Center. Alan had a pretty good idea of which direction to take, but the kids were tired and couldn't walk very fast.

As the sun set, they walked through an open field. In the distance the T-rex roared.

"I think we'd better find a place to spend the night," Alan said. He looked around for a safe place and decided that a tall tree would be best. "Let's climb up here," he said.

The T-rex roared again.

"Now!"

The kids climbed up first and Alan followed, giving them a push when they needed one. They settled in, each child snuggled on one side of Alan.

The view from the tree was amazing. The park stretched for miles and was lit up by moonlight. They could see dinosaurs in the open fields. The Brachiosaur heads towered above everything.

In the morning, Alan, Tim, and Lex were sleeping comfortably in the tree while the sun shone brightly above them. Then a heavy shadow fell over all three of them, blocking out the sun completely. A giant Brachiosaur's head poked through the branches and began

to chomp on some nearby leaves. Everyone woke at once.

Lex opened her mouth to scream but nothing came out. She moved away from the dinosaur.

"Veggiesaurus, Lex," Tim said as he climbed up to a higher branch to give the beast a friendly pat. "It won't hurt you." The Brachiosaur continued eating while Tim petted its head.

Alan grabbed the dinosaur's lips and pulled them down to examine its mouth. "Come on over, Lex," Alan said. "Just think of it as a big cow."

Reluctantly, Lex moved closer to the animal. When she was right in front of its head she reached out and touched it lightly on the nose. Suddenly, the dinosaur sneezed, covering Lex from head to toe with slime.

"Eeeewwww," Lex said, wiping her face in disgust.

Just then a strange animal cry came from off in the distance and the Brachiosaur moved quickly away from the tree.

Lex, Tim, and Alan climbed down.

"Look!" Alan cried out, alarmed. He was pointing to a thin white piece of shell that lay on the ground.

"What is it?" Tim asked.

"It looks like a piece of dinosaur egg!"

Alan answered, picking it up. He noticed a trail of little white pieces and followed it to the other side of the tree. There, in front of him, was a whole clutch of hatched dinosaur eggs. Everyone's eyes grew wide.

The dinosaurs *couldn't* all be female. They were breeding! And soon all of Jurassic Park would be out of control!

In the control room, Mr. Hammond had made an important decision.

"The fences are all off. Everything is off," he said. "Things are out of control. We have to shut down the entire system.

It's the only way to undo what Nedry has done."

Ray Arnold couldn't believe what he was hearing. The system had never been completely turned off. It was a huge risk. But he also knew that they didn't really have a choice. It would clear the system and when they switched it back on, the park would be in working order again.

If everything went the way it was supposed to.

Ray stood up and walked over to a metal box on the wall. He opened it and flipped a row of switches. Finally, he flipped a large lever, and the room went black.

Everyone waited in silent darkness.

"How long do we wait?" Ellie asked.

"About ten seconds," Ray answered. Then he flipped the row of switches back on. His hand moved slowly toward the lever, and he flipped that, too.

Nothing happened.

Nobody said anything. Then Ray remembered something and ran to the computer. "It worked!" he shouted. "Look." The computer screen said *system ready.* "We just have to get to the maintenance shed and turn the breakers back on," Ray explained.

"Let's go," Robert Muldoon said.

Alan, Lex, and Tim walked through the park grounds. In the distance they heard dinosaur calls.

Alan studied a map he had with him. "The Visitor's Center should be just about a mile from here," he said. "We're almost there."

The animal sounds seemed to be all around them and were getting louder. It almost seemed as if more and more dinosaurs were joining in. Alan peered into the distance. He could just make out shapes—moving shapes. Dinosaurs! Dozens of them.

There was a rumbling, and all at once Alan realized what it was: a dinosaur stampede. And it was heading right for them!

"Run!" Alan shouted as the T-rex stormed out of the jungle, surprising the stampeding dinosaurs. Alan, Lex, and Tim took off across the meadow, running as fast as they could.

"Under here!" Alan pointed to a giant cluster of roots, and the three scrambled below, just as the dinosaurs thundered overhead.

Through the roots they watched as the T-rex chased down a Gallimimus and sunk its teeth into the dinosaur's neck.

Lex saw her chance to get away— while the T-rex was busy. "Let's go!" she yelled, standing up.

Alan and Tim didn't move, though. They were transfixed by the T-rex.

"Well, *I'm* going." She ran off, and Alan and Tim tore themselves away and followed her.

Ellie and Robert grabbed some guns and started across the compound to the maintenance shed. As they passed the Velociraptor pen, they stopped dead in their tracks. There was a hole in the fence. The Raptors were on the loose!

Out of the corner of his eye Robert saw something move in the dense jungle. Suddenly he realized that he and Ellie were being watched—hunted. "Raptors," he said quietly. "I'll distract them. You just get to the shed and flip the breaker switches."

"Okay." Ellie ran to the shed, burst through the door, and slammed it behind her.

DANGER
10,000
VOLTS

Meanwhile, Alan, Tim, and Lex scrambled through the forest, exhausted. "We're almost there," Alan assured them.

Finally, they came to the huge electrified fence that surrounded the main compound. They were almost home. Lex and Tim collapsed on the ground.

Alan looked up at the fence, which was at least twenty feet high. "It's not on," he said, looking at the blank computer monitor at the top. "It's safe to climb. Think you guys can make it?"

"Nope," said Tim.

"It's way too high," Lex agreed.

Then a deafening roar rang through the jungle. Both kids jumped to their feet and started to climb.

Alan climbed the fence faster than the kids, and just before he reached the ground he saw a warning light flash. Someone was turning the fence on! "Get off the fence," he yelled to the kids. "*Now!*"

Lex climbed down quickly, but Tim froze near the top.

The warning light flashed faster.

"Tim, you have to let go!" Alan shouted. "I'll catch you."

"No, I can make it," Tim insisted.

Ellie found the main switch in the control box and flipped it. The fence surged with high-voltage power, and Tim screamed as he fell to the ground.

Back in the maintenance shed, Ellie's flashlight pierced the darkness. She carefully made her way down the metal stairs and along a corridor until she found the aluminum control box.

If she could just get the power back on, the electric fences and all the computers would work again. There might be a chance for everyone in Jurassic Park to survive.

The lights in the maintenance shed came on suddenly, and Ellie found herself face-to-face with a Raptor! For a second it just stared at her with its sharp eyes. Then, in a flash, it lunged. Ellie screamed and ran for the staircase, the snarling Raptor at her heels. Just as the Raptor was gaining on her, she threw open the door and escaped into the daylight.

Meanwhile, Robert Muldoon crept slowly through the jungle. He'd decided to go after the Raptor he'd seen earlier.

The Raptor moved farther and farther into the foliage. Then it stopped and moved into view. Robert smiled as he lifted his gun and took aim. But then the smile faded. This was too easy. Where were the other Raptors? Was he being hunted from the side or behind? Just then the Raptors attacked. No one could help him now.

"Timmy!" Lex ran to her brother. He lay on the ground, not breathing, his face white. "Oh, *no!*" she cried.

Alan leaned over Tim's still body, examining him. Then he began to do CPR, alternating compressions on the chest with breaths over his mouth.

"Come on," Alan murmured.

Finally, Tim gasped and came to. Lex wrapped her brother's burned hands in a piece of Alan's shirt. Alan picked him up and carried him to the Visitor's Center.

The Visitor's Center was dark and spooky. "Hello?" Alan called. There was no answer. Maybe things were worse than they had thought.

Alan took the kids to the cafeteria and got them settled at a table. "I'm just going to find the others," he said. "You'll be safe as long as you stay here."

Lex nodded as she watched Alan head out the cafeteria door.

Tim was slumped in a chair. He looked terrible.

"Are you hungry?" Lex asked him.

Tim just shrugged, but Lex got a plateful of food for him anyway. She sat down across from him and spooned up some Jell-O. Then she saw something move. "Tim," her voice shook. "Something's here."

They turned to look at the huge glass mural of dinosaurs and saw a *real* Raptor shadow moving behind it.

Lex frantically threw an arm around Tim and helped him into the kitchen. Breathing hard, she closed the door and helped her brother hide behind one of the rows of steel cabinets.

From their hiding place, Lex and Tim could see the Raptor. It stood outside, looking through the little window in the door. Then it pounded its head against the door.

While Lex and Tim watched in horror, the door handle began to turn slowly. The Raptor was discovering how to open the door! A moment later the door opened and the Raptor stepped into the kitchen. Then another Raptor appeared—there were two of them!

Each Raptor took a different direction. They were hunting, just like they

would have in the prehistoric jungle.

Lex crawled toward the kitchen door, away from the Raptors. Tim followed, but he was so tired he could barely move. And when he brushed up against a rack of kitchen utensils, the clanging noise gave him away. The Raptors came after him in a flash.

Quickly, Lex grabbed a spoon off a counter and began to tap it on the stone floor. The strange clicking attracted the Raptors, and they moved toward it.

Tim was exhausted, but when he spotted a walk-in freezer on the far wall, a plan suddenly came to him. He knew what he had to do.

As one of the Raptors closed in on Lex, she looked for a place to hide. She crawled into a cabinet, but it was too late. The Raptor had seen her. It crouched down, ready to spring.

THUD! The Raptor crashed—into the wrong cabinet! It had been fooled by Lex's reflection on another shiny metal cabinet. Stunned, it fell to the floor.

Tim saw his chance and made a break for the freezer. He got to the door, pulled it open, and threw himself inside. It was freezing, and the floor was icy. Tim slipped just as the other Raptor came through the door behind him. The vicious dinosaur slipped and fell, too.

There was a moment of confusion, and Tim saw Lex at the door. He scrambled toward her and slipped out of the freezer to safety. The Raptor screamed as Lex slammed the freezer door in its snarling face.

On their way out of the kitchen, Tim and Lex ran into Alan and Ellie. Alan picked Tim up and together they hurried into the control room.

While Lex and Ellie worked at the main computer, Alan set Tim down in a chair and went to secure the control room door. But the system hadn't been turned on and the door wouldn't lock.

Suddenly, something rammed against the outside of the door. A Raptor!

"Quick," Alan shouted, "get the door locks back on!"

Ellie ran to help him hold the door while Lex's fingers flew over the computer keyboard. The Raptor threw itself against the door again and again. Alan and Ellie leaned against the door with all of their weight but they couldn't hold it shut forever.

Finally, Lex found the right command, executed it, and the lock clicked. The Raptor was locked outside.

A few moments later Ellie screamed. Another Raptor was trying to get in from the outside!

Alan looked around in a panic. There was nowhere to go—nowhere except up. "The ceiling!" he shouted. "Let's go!"

In a flash the Raptor burst into the control room through the window. Glass

flew everywhere. But the room was already empty. Alan and Ellie were leading the kids through the crawl space above the ceiling.

The Raptor watched the ceiling move for a second. Then it struck. It jumped straight up, bursting through one of the ceiling panels and snapping its powerful jaws.

"Into the air duct!" Alan shouted, pointing ahead.

Just then the Raptor jumped again, right underneath Lex. For a moment she was pinned between the Raptor's head and the ceiling above. And when the Raptor fell back down, Lex fell with it!

"Help!" she screamed.

At the last moment Alan grabbed her by the collar and yanked her back up.

Alan, Ellie, and the kids scrambled through the air duct. They could hear the snarling Raptor somewhere behind them, but it was hard to tell how far back it was.

Suddenly they saw a light. It was coming through a metal grate in the air duct. Alan could see the unfinished lobby of the Visitor's Center below. But they were too far above the floor to jump.

Alan pulled the grate up and jumped onto some scaffolding. Then he climbed onto the towering skeleton of the Brachiosaur. "Come on," he said. "We can climb down this way."

The kids climbed carefully onto the dinosaur skeleton. Then Ellie followed.

But as soon as she let go of the scaffolding, the bolts that held the skeleton to the ceiling started to come loose.

"We can make it," Alan said. "Just keep moving."

The sound of claws on metal echoed through the Visitor's Center, and the Raptor came exploding out of the air duct.

"Hurry!" Alan shouted as the Raptor thudded onto the scaffolding. But it was too late. The Raptor leaped, landing on the Brachiosaur neck just above them. It coiled its body, preparing to spring at them.

Suddenly the bolts in the ceiling ripped free and the Brachiosaur skeleton collapsed in a heap, taking everyone with it.

Alan, Ellie, and the kids pulled themselves up. "Let's go!" Alan shouted, pointing toward the main exit. But then he saw the other Raptor—the biggest one, the leader of the pack. It was standing right in the doorway. There was no escape.

A dark shadow fell over all of the lobby and a massive head swung down. The T-rex! It bit into the big Raptor, lifted it high into the air, and threw it to the ground.

Just then Mr. Hammond and Ian Malcolm pulled up to the Visitor's Center in a Jeep. Alan and the others ran to it. As they climbed inside, the T-rex attacked the last Raptor, ripping it in half.

"I've called for a helicopter," Mr. Hammond said as they sped away from the Visitor's Center. "It's on its way."

With everyone safely inside, the rescue helicopter lifted into the sky, leaving Jurassic Park behind. Mr. Hammond never opened his park, and nobody goes to the island anymore. But the native people of Costa Rica still tell stories. And secrets may still lie hidden in the misty fog that covers Isla Nublar.